Norman Pinglepop

Story of a usual GOD

notionpress.com

Norman Pinglepop

Story of a usual GOD

Jasmeet Chhabra

notionpress.com

Notion Press

5 Muthu Kalathy Street, Triplicane,

Chennai - 600 005

First Published by Notion Press 2015

ISBN: 978-93-84878-58-0

Preface

GODHOOD as a concept had often intrigued me through growing up years and still continues to be an enigma that has taken me through many journeys resting with Viapassana[1] which finally appealed to my experiential self as a path then just a means to a mental construct.

Norman Pinglepop is a satire that in a dark manner expresses the long and deep distrust religions, dogmas and doctrines caste in my mind over the years in the garb of a benign power construed as GOD but driven by infirm emotions that drive us humans. It often confused me, how can GOD conduct commerce with his benevolence, if he was all powerful, and then the desire to sift through the motivation of godhood for subservience and GODHOOD for surrender got me to Norman Pinglepop.

---

1 Vipassana - A meditation technique in the order of Late Shir S.N.Goenkaji (URL: www.dhamma.org)

Prologue

There are two kinds of freedom. The true freedom, where we do what we ought to do and the illusionary freedom where we do what we wish to do. In the latter, we are often enslaved to the pleasures of our senses and the web of our conditioning and hence what is often acted upon is that which suits us in ill- taste.

This however, is not visible to the naked eye as it is often dressed in fancy and eulogized in the garb of sacrifice, martyrdom, heroism, chivalry and all else fancy sounding expressions.

I have often wondered at the futility of patriotism dependent on simply protecting the borders of a state while allowing all acts of treason and adultery to be committed inside those realms.

Would I respond to the call for sacrifice when I know that all I am expected to be is but a poor feedstock for someone's ambition here or foolery there? And yet the world is agog with the stories of those who live and die for the sake of physical boundaries even as they themselves fall prey to the deterioration in values and morals within.

In the light of this ill- fitting freedom, how is it that man has given up on thinking? To still romanticize a zombie's existence, ha, alas!

This false freedom then forms the basis of power. The power that plays on the sentiment and rules by the brawn of a dying head, devoid of reason and oblivious to the bounty that he hides under a bushel so well.

The comfort of numbness goes a long way in making lives miserable and then in the honest attempt at witch hunting, fate is the next casualty in the blame game.

Norman Pinglepop

I am not Norman Pinglepop! I am not Norman Pinglepop…

But does it matter anymore to the hungry hounds? For them, I am Norman Pinglepop and now, they will pounce on me and tear my skin… suck my blood and cast my intestines away for the lesser dogs to prey.

The very thought of it churns my entire system in a frenzy and I am thinking, "Why did I have to pretend like Norman Pinglepop" and now, all the glory of those days will return in wounded pride to haunt me, to hunt me.

Norman Pinglepop! The first time I heard the name, even I was a little surprised. Yet the reverence he received from these **Marsh Dwellers** was amazing. Then, one day, he just vanished. Ever since, they have made him their GOD.

It's only little co-incidence then that they mistook me for him and before I could speak I was already atop the pedestal, the hero of a lost race for a futile cause, a hero nevertheless. Now that I look back it seems so easy… No, we did not look alike, nor did we have anything in common. I guess it's just that my **Marsh Dwellers** were tired of waiting and decided that Godlike Norman Pinglepop had taken a new form to awe his humble subjects.

Laura always looked at me with suspicion. Having known the humility of her people, she had reasons to doubt me. After all, I hardly conducted myself like the divine Pinglepop. I was known to swear on the slightest provocation and I could drink like there was no tomorrow and flirt like my virility would be wasted if left unused.

Now, Laura was like the sunlight on a chilly morning. Need I say more? It was love at first sight. I have reasons to believe it was more of lust, and when she would not give in to my whims, it took on the sheen of divine love. But that is between us and discretion is often the better part of valor.

Oh GOD! Let no GOD ever drink in excess and better still, let not the love of his life stand in front of his lustful drunken self. On hindsight, I think Laura knew I was vulnerable! Otherwise, she would not have smiled so much at my wavering composure.

Laura was a fine woman with slender fingers, voluptuous breasts, childlike curiosity, whimsical manners and an absolutely nonchalant manly walk. But considering, she was three-four inches taller then me, I never got to see much of the walk or the manners… just the fingers at times… when they would obstruct my view.

She would often ask me of my days as the original Norman Pinglepop. I have reasons to believe that she was in love with him. Even as the reverence of the entire **Marshy** populace forbade her from unveiling my "treason", she would often corner me with an embarrassing smile, having caught me ignorant about my own identity (read Norman Pinglepop).

It was a strange revelation and I had never seen this form of her before. Laura was an imposing façade drowned in opium and there she stood right in front of me, half bare, half curious and now staring. Like a prey in the path of a prowling heartless carnivore, she pounced on me. "I am not a fool," she said.

"Run for your dear life before the villagers pelt you to death. How could you even think of dishonoring our Lord the GOD, Norman Pinglepop? "

Satanically speaking, her vain hollering would not make much difference. After all, to belittle my existence would be to belittle the existence of the very man who defined GODHOOD for them. Have you ever wondered what would happen to their miniscule lives if their GOD died in disgrace? For a moment I felt secure in this blanket of logic. Then the evil brain-now awake from a blundering charade-got me wondering,

"I am not Norman Pinglepop! But, who is Laura?"

I mean what is GOD without that beautiful, tempting, much desired incarnation called Evil? What is the value of sacrifice if there be no temptation demanding sacrifice for cleansing? Of course, we created the sins and the sinners to keep the prophets on the job or they would have spat their lungs out begging for alms.

This sudden strange smile, now turning to mirth, now to contempt, must have scared Laura. She gave me those funny looks again. I say 'again' since I look at her face afresh and am wondering if they were always there. Just that I never noticed anything about her, apart from those fingers and the slender hand when it would obstruct my view sometimes.

So the stage was set. Laura the heretic, Laura the bewitched, the charmed was now my equivalent of Lucifer thrown out of favor from the kingdom of Our Father in the forest - I mean Norman Pinglepop, if you have not already guessed by now!

My loud laughter roared through her ears and she stood their feigning courage where there was none left and I, displaying rage, as I tried hard to control this tickle in my throat created by my majestically loud roar. I had often wanted to work in the village theatre group and now I was playing GOD.

Laura left and I had nothing else left to see that evening. I dedicated the evening to measly attempts at making up, following the paths, which Laura had traced into the village.

I am living an ideology tonight and the fruits of perseverance are my last hope. This dilemma - Ahem! To be a hero, the legendary Norman Pinglepop, and stay till the forest beckons; then perish to be another form incarnate. Or, do I stand and see my gutless stomach belch with the poison of staring eyes galore? I do have this urgent need to speak the truth like Coelho's ace magus[2] who made a sacred promise to undo all that he would ever do.

Why is it that, what is, is seldom enough and what is not, is seldom achieved? This satiated tempest alas! I feel this vigor flowing down my bile, and soon the spleen will poison the last remnants of sanity in me. These lofty ideals that you make me live up to, and the ease with which you make me the exception to the same ideals, sometimes surprises me. You pray to the same GOD, who imposes penury on you and ask for penance. How bizarre are the ways of men, wanting so hard to draw reason into sepulchers of a dying custom, a dead tradition, all bound together in another nude show of static void.

Laura came back to me today. I saw the hurt in her eyes- the anger of an empress now drawn to dust. I know she would never fancy trusting me, but her bewilderment is now her weapon. She often questions her GOD… How

---

2 *The Pilgrimage by Paulo Coelho*

is it that her truth is lesser then my farce? And her GOD is now tied down to my body and his soul finds voice no more?

I will lead her to my bed in compromise of the defamation that she dared cause me. I will win her over through the bestiality in us mortals and will nurture venom for the GOD that forsook her. I will fill her with the appendage of my own belittled pleasures and enslave her senses to the wasted alcoholic who seldom feels the pleasure but in pain. Until one day, her subdued self will rise in strike and ask for her due. I hope I am still alive that day because then, I will make her my GOD.

Am I again trying my hand at nobility? Norman Pinglepop is dead and I am a mere heretic. As long as I know this, I will never be true to you. And the illusion of our world deems it fit that we live in a bigger lie, each time we seek the truth.

There is this sinister plan. I remember that in the inebriated night of yesterday, I had visions of being powerful. In any case, this peace is not my idea of GODHOOD. What is it that I control when there is hardly a thing left to control? So much order and so much numbness can cause my authority to explode at the first signs of external miscreant.

No, not Laura… the Devil has to come later. What comes first is the proof of belief of the make-believe followers. So now, I will put them to test and seek miracles if they exist or at best the blood of the innocent to wash their altar of my sins.

Ever wondered? Why are the dead always innocent and good departed souls? I guess it's about time I found that out for myself…

So I choose **Marshy Moron** for my minister for propaganda. His name is rhetoric for the acts of omission he will dramatize as his commission. We the **Marsh Dwellers** are now set to expand our sect and the realm of influence of our GOD- the legendary Norman Pinglepop. We will conquer the green heights of the **Mountain Mosquitoers** and then steer our victory march to the **Amphibiotic Ambivalent** before descending on the **Valley of the Ignorants.**

To lead the attack, I have appointed, **Callous Concoction**s and his drunken army. They will lead the front and disparage their way through the tender souls of men and will intoxicate their sanity till the weak follow and the strong bow to the whims of Us- the GOD race.

The days are filled with frenzy, we all have a new sense of purpose and we are doing our existences some justice finally. I peep through the windows on some nights and I hear men talking of valor and death by the sword as though it is some type of heroism to pledge your dear life for the sake of ideals that have risen from our own meager heads. But I am not complaining.

In some places, there is gloom of the impending martyrdom and the **Marsh Dwellers** are a more serious lot now than when they lost their GOD Norman Pinglepop. That they found me is somehow their comfort because I have apparently come back from the forest after finding my salvation they fancy as their own. My purpose now, fills these hollow men.

The pre-war preparations breed a new hero in **Marshy Moron**. The tales of valor and wisdom that he spins out of mere disdain for the losing sense of common existence, at times make me wonder in amusement at the gullibility of my race and at others, scares me so I get up in fright to take notice of the lesser legion becoming an "alter GOD".

Thankfully, **Marshy Moron** is dutifully dedicated to me, and his conditioning spans longer than my entire life. So I am confident that he will give his life for me even as I take his to save mine.

The forces are gradually becoming more impassioned and now that women and children have been added to the holy war, the caste and creed distinctions that were once a fashion here, no longer exist. That only adds to my comfort and well, another feather in my cap. Wondering if it makes me a bigger GOD! Hail Norman Pinglepop!

Callous Concoctions had never felt so important in life before. Never had so many people been at his foot, ready to die at his command. He is a grateful old braggart and often, I hear him brag of me in an attempt to prove how servile a slave he is to the GOD of the masses. I sometimes wonder how we set our own limits and our own standards and one fine day, die with them.

But **Callous Concoction** has to live since I have already planned a death for him. The one that will make him an eternal martyr after his last victory. That way, he will not have to carry the guilt of his success to his grave and hence, will not command jeers during future inactivity.

Meanwhile, I have the need for my Lady Lucifer again. Laura has been away for a while. I think she saw what was in store for her and decided to go seek solutions in the forest, hoping her Norman Pinglepop- her GOD would be there. While her absence is a relief as I brew this storm, now in its full ripe form, it needs the dressing of that perfect taster of men.

I often loathed witch hunting. But today, I realize that, in the relative world, the only means we have inherited of growing taller is to stand in the company of dwarfs. I choose to outgrow mortality and to achieve my GODHOOD. Laura shall be my mortal vile company.

Marshy Moron does not quite understand the truce but his deft agile fingers are already at work, writing the "Fatwa" to find Laura the heretic, alive or broken, but not dead. **Callous Concoction** has also sent his band of the most able men in search of the mean little thing… oops! I mean my petite Lucifer – Laura.

Meanwhile, the frontline of the attack team has to be enhanced.

I see a man often walk up to me in humble subservience, but his eyes often betray their true purpose. Sometimes, I single him out of the others and he feels really important. He has often, in such moments, pledged his life to my service and at others, feigned ignorance and went around town slandering the very essence of GOD. I feel a need for this two-edged sword now.

Mucus Migraine is his name and henceforth, he is the chief architect of the sleaze society. Times have given its seal of approval to victories, often overlooking the games waged for the victory.

Mucus Migraine will spread the virus of malice in those loving races that have long lived together, brew discontent amongst the **Amphibiotic Ambivalent** and dare the **Mountain Mosquitoers** to a show of valor against their own brethren. Women will play the heretic in the innocent desire for control, often battered by Christian morality.

But for the **Valley of Ignorance** where I am afraid I might meet Babylon, albeit in a more prolonged sense of time than did Alexander the Great, the battle will be played on a different field.

Ignorance has often been the best weapon of mankind in his wisest form. For, to knowledge is owed fear and to fear, the need for an identity and to identity, our false purpose of selfhood, which can be dared to, enslaved or led to self destruction. But the ignorant often stay out of this little treason that makes heroes and villains out of conditioned races.

The Valley has the balm to frustrate **Mucus Migraine** and his sleaze, the simplicity to simply not comprehend **Marshy Moron** and his often quasi-real calls for a brave death and **Callous Concoction**'s misdemeanor by their self-proclaimed surrender.

While this surrender often leads us to illusions of easy victory, yet it deprives the diabolical thrill of a rape which is often lost in gentle lovemaking and for a masquerading marauder like Callous, this will be a sure invitation to self extinction.

So, the blueprint for the Great War for ethnic cleansing is laid, with a few gray spots still appearing. We feel confident of winning over the **Mosquitoers** and the **Ambivalents** but the **Ignorants** are still to be tackled and the search for the suitable man stares at me squarely yet again. The only reason I can think of the mantle falling on me is that there is nothing special about me.

Of course, this apart, the borrowed GODHOOD should make the **Ignorants** look up in haste to the historical moment, when I visit them and at that moment, I hope to be able to force a strike. However, I keep the plan to myself for now and let the summons for valor and vanity play havoc by the sword of the brave and th pen of the grave.

Celebrations are now a norm at the **Marsh Land**, and the pomp and glamour that have the wings to carry it far and wide, with an aptly built in debate is now making out-roads to the rest of the world.

It was a brilliant moment of awakening and the moment still flashes in my head, even as the outcome of each of those moments sometimes overwhelms me with fear and at other times lifts my spirits like a genius.

Men have a desperate need to doubt their worth, which is then hidden in the altars of GOD or the arms of intoxication. While one often takes refuge in wisdom, the other takes the form of guilt and lingers in its strange reproductive habitat.

The idea was simple. With a little help from **Marshy Moron** and **Mucus Migraine**, we developed the propaganda vehicle. The message was to be mixed with festivities, which would give an aura of elation to our blokes, and the thought police of the sleaze gang was to instill the desired guilt by doubting the very existence of their GOD- the redoubtable Norman Pinglepop.

This led to long bouts of verbal conflicts followed by physical violence to cool down. And at the end of it all, the festivities would start again.

Marsh Land became the enigmatic new world of a unique creation where nothing ever existed in black or white- except in the minds of the director of the stage. With the percolation of gray in the grey cells of an otherwise sleepy race, the resultant confusion was but the material, legends are made of in far off lands.

I am told the **Mosquitoers** were already feeling threatened within months of this cultural uprisings. Nowhere had the **Mosquitoers** believed that the sad, sleepy **Marsh Dwellers** would someday match their glory and infamy (or notoriety) in one breath. And here they were, looking them in the eye.

While violence in my name grew, my popularity and immortality grew at a faster rate. After all, I was not just their GOD now, but their leader, their path maker who was slowly and steadily leading them to a life of grandeur amongst their distant brethren.

The central character amongst the mortals in the entire uprisings was **Callous Concoction**. Since men of ordinary sand do not become Gods and Lords in one lifetime, they then aspire to be the man closest to their idea of authority, power and self-righteous glory. It is another story that this self-righteous glory calls for many a sacrifice of the even lesser mortals. After all, logic has always approved of sacrifices of a village for a city and a city for a country and so on and so forth.

The sleaze club made a hero of **Callous** while calling me names. Yet, the propaganda army of **Marshy Moron** indulged lavishly in **Callous**-bashing to protect my sainthood.

While the results-as I have already touched upon-were more than satisfactory, yet the growing popularity of **Callous** would be of concern to me.

But this was not a worry to last long. Soon I had the mist washed off my morning and in clearer rays of the afternoon sun, I carefully planned the path to martyrdom for our dear **Callous.** By evening, I could almost feel the ruddy drops of red in the sinking sun, flowing out of **Callous'** body taking petty precious life with them on the *charmed stage of martyrdom.*

Next morning, the incredible stage was set. The **Marsh Dwellers** in their finest best were all out on the streets to see their hero **Callous** mount his horse to wage the first ever onslaught on the **Mountain Mosquitoers**. The colors of valor in saffron and of grief in white, camouflaged in burning incandescence and the faithful in the Green Army bid their final adieu to their families on their path to martyrdom.

If they returned victorious, why, the celebrations would be replaced with even more celebrations? If they died on the battlefield, we will erect altars in their names and vow to fight again to avenge their deaths. Having done that, we will rejoice in festivities at having found a new purpose for our frugal existence.

Mucus Migraine had already done his bit at raising **Callous** to the priesthood, befitting a true servant of GOD. Up to the borders of **Marsh Land** there were banners solemnly pledging support of the local village to the almighty **Callous**. At every checkpoint, hundreds of faithful gathered in Green to offer their bit of sacrifice to **Callous** before retiring to their daily chores.

While **Mucus** and his sleaze army ensured that the war would be won before it began by reinforcing the trust and confidence of the **Marsh Dwellers**, and dispelling all hopes with a pall of gloom over the **Mountain Mosquitoers**, **Marshy Moron** was preparing for the ultimate Martyrdom.

In the ensuing month of severe fighting, the balances tripped many times towards and away from **Callous**. Alas! The **Mosquitoers** were vastly underestimated by our Generals' concocted view of the situation. The imageries of a grand homecoming that had filled **Callous'** vision on his way to the war were the only hope that kept him alive and fighting.

The war was finally won in our favor. **Mucus Migraine** and his sleaze club joined **Callous'** drunken army in plundering and looting the **Mountain Mosquiters**. Arson and forced conversions became the order of the day. But we did not intervene. The seat of Norman Pinglepop neither accepted, nor acknowledged the savagery unleashed by God's derailed followers.

While **Marshy Moron** was testing the waters to see the reaction of the **Marsh Dwellers** to the entire episode, he often-exploded into statistical laughter at the naiveté of the poor **Marsh Dwellers**. While his attack on the immorality of **Callous** ensured guilt in them, the victory of **Callous** nurtured the savage in turn and they were often caught between the virtues of victories and the pain of being self- righteous.

Then one day, we heard from **Callous** about his victory march back home. The stage was now set for the final attack. **Marshy Moron** and his propaganda machinery were now in full throttle planning the royal martyrdom of **Callous**.

A series of events ensued between the first information provided by **Callous** and the time the **Marsh Dwellers** would learn about the homecoming of their Hero.

The man who had done an entire tribe proud by making them one with the victorious was now returning and the euphoria was but obvious. Only this time, their Euphoria was not induced. What instead was added to spice the celebrations were a few instances of violence and a lot many, of plots and treacheries.

Marshy Moron was indeed a genius in his game. From the murder of a few innocents to an attempted murder of Norman Pinglepop, their GOD, everything was carried out with immaculate élan and the vote of majority so that all the lies were now the only truths.

After the garlands and the warm welcomes into the open arms of gullible maidens, **Callous Concoction** was finally murdered a few miles from the gates of the capital city where he was coming to offer his victories and his mission to their GOD.

The gloom that followed was taken in their stride by the enduring, persevering and the new heroes of another lost world, the **Marsh Dwellers**, in parts shaken by the mortality of their Lord and in parts, intimidated by the written words splashed across the country by **Marshy Moron**.

It was my time to offer condolences to the Hero I had once created and give him his rightful burial, which, I, Norman Pinglepop, did with a tear in my eyes and the stern words of a stoic in my speeches.

Marsh Dwellers had finally found a hero amongst themselves which elevated their GOD to a superior status of unimpeachable stature while they would now contend themselves with measuring up to the highest amongst men- **Callous Concoction-** without ever having to be accountable to his living self.

There is some satisfaction in making ideals out of mortals. I think its called convenience.

Stage one of my plan had succeeded. But there was no time to rest and we had to move on. It often reminded me of Robert Frost and his "The Woods are lovely dark and deep, but I have promises to keep" in my new sense of purpose.

Our next campaign would be against the **Amphibiotic Ambivalent** but before that, my **Marsh Dwellers** need to rejoice in the heroic victory of their general **Callous** and mourn over his untimely death. They also need to be introduced to the devil in absentia, their own Laura… to complete their conviction of sphere-e-city of life…

Ever wondered if it is valor that survives propaganda or the other way round. It has been just thirteen days since the heroic martyrdom of **Callous** and our friend **Marshy Moron** has already identified seventy-three potential conduits who may be framed for his brutal murder from time to time, depending on the mood of our people and/ or the need of the hour.

The list is a well-evaluated mix of diplomats, nobles of our enemy kingdoms (who are now regrouping in the face of impending danger) and common folk who may be raised to the stature of heroes or anti- heroes to keep the fizz alive in the futile purposefulness of our distinguished publics.

Mucus Migraine has also been able to successfully display the power of paranoia by inducing the hitherto alien concepts of spirits and the fallen heroes by identifying people who hold their loyalties to the convict in absentia, Laura. The Lucifer loyalists unknown to their own purpose shall be exposed in the most unassuming manner. So unassuming is the entire affair planned to be that even they would not know when they become the anecdotes to dawn upon the black book of treachery.

Sometimes the power of their minds puts me to wonderment... **Mucus** and **Moron** both seem to be such excellent readers of men that I fear someday I shall also be read. And I am glad since this awareness makes me paranoid and keeps me alert all the time, which in such times is the better part of valor.

Given to the power of twin evils of sleaze and farce, a man's mind can be a fertile breeding ground for bizarre obedience and dissent at the same time. I guess the secret lies in misdirection. To make someone believe he is the hero and then decree his obedience, which he shall gladly obey for fear of losing his heroism.

Callous Concoction is dead and the city center now harbors a huge sculpture of his victorious march. After a few days of celebrations at the square, the crows and pigeons now adorn his mighty gait. They let their droppings decorate his aspect and make love by the night on his mighty sword.

Soon they would have built their comfortable nests to hatch their young ones and finally **Callous** would look up from heaven and smile at his folly of valor and now look down upon his lesser-known cousin of noble use. So what if it is for the pigeons and crows of his GOD's kingdom?

My **Marsh Dwellers** are yet not decided whether their mighty general was really that mighty or was he just a figment of their imagination and once again I can scarcely stop to admire the dual virtues of **Moron** and **Mucus**… this diabolique duality ahem!

But there is no time to be wasted now and the numb comfort needs to be shaken by another cry of valor. The **Marsh Dwellers** do not hold ambition as one of their greatest virtue unlike their Lord Norman Pinglepop and hence need to be prodded to this subtle art of self-destruction.

I see this strange pattern of self-righteousness also breeding form. I am sure the heretics of Laura are at the game now. The fortunate dwellers of the Lord's own country are taking their fortune a bit too seriously I am told! They would not let another head fall or another drop of blood be shed; all this because they suddenly see themselves as the "protecting" race".

This breeds ill omen here. But alas! I loved Laura; I did… at least whatever I saw of her. Which is not speaking much-upwards of her torso-but at least she is well endowed and what a pity it would be to let it go waste! To celebrate the spirit of heresy that I shall soon endow her with. Then again, there is a price for everything I guess.

The battle of the **Amphibiatic Ambivalents** was not to be won by the sword. The **Ambivalents** have a pact of self-destruction, which would bring them of their own fear and wisdom, to my feet.

So for the time being, I need to concentrate on the home turf. Knowledge corrupts and absolute knowledge corrupts absolutely. What is a man without the eternal struggle of good and evil, right and wrong? We don't need a thinking race in the country of GOD! Just a bunch of headless followers and that needs the eternal strife of good and evil alike.

Mucus surprised me by reading my thoughts and speaking them aloud. His sleaze sometimes gets to my nerves but I have to keep this straight face for he is very very perceptive.

While **Moron** has been doing a wonderful job of gathering all the intelligence that he finds befitting for his GOD to know, it is **Mucus** who can see the danger in the self-righteous rebellion in **Marsh Land**.

In his drunken best, his ambitions speak better than his actions, and in one such moment of vulnerability he had told me about the brilliant idea of incriminating Laura.

After all, the astute among the **Marsh Dwellers** knew of Laura and her liking to their LORD. And now they can smell her opposition to their victorious GOD. Hence it would not be difficult to declare her the villain for all the worthy causes. That ways, the spirit of limited faculties that a man so loves to tie himself down to would stay alive and our people will have something to feed their self doubting eulogies.

Mucus chose the best of the lot in his sleaze party and they were his champions in Laura's camp. They started off by being the perfect followers till they could find out the breach in her line of command. It did not take them longer then a month to be the most trusted lieutenants of the **Noble Warriors** led by Laura.

Thereafter they started to fill with sleaze, the source of inspiration that was the basis of her movement.

Laura had never stopped to surprise me but that evening when **Mucus** in his triumphant best brought to me the "Fatwa" that she would be reading out to her **Noble Warriors,** to wage on all out war against the imposter in the garb of their GOD… I was humbled.

The "Fatwa" read, "Noble men of **Marsh Land**! Rise!

The imposter has usurped the throne of our holy GOD and fed us the stupor of grandeur in valiant death. But our

Lord the true Norman Pinglepop believed in freedom of will and mind.

The imposter has sold us the dreams of victory when all that one ever needs to win over is the heart within, the soul within… what victory it is that we buy with blood of our brethren.

To defeat a fellow human race goes beyond the basic instinct of survival that inspires a carnivore to predate his prey. It is, but a mean feat of a weak mind, which needs the garb of ambition to hide its impotency and the garlands of victory to hide the insecurity of a worthless living.

There is no GOD who would lead his men to bloodshed and rejoice on the color of crimson. We all are but inhabitants of this Mother Earth and we all are here to LIVE… not to kill.

Yet this imposter intoxicates us with misdirection and caters to the infirmity of purpose… **Noble Warriors** rise… for we had found our GOD in Ignorance and in Ignorance is where he lives!

For the true soul follows the thoughtless- thought being but a slave to illusions, which conditioning has gifted us as legacy of its own failings.

We have found our GOD and he does not impose his authority. Though, his authority is supreme. It needs no reason in bloodshed and victory and it needs no reason in our guilt and heroic misdemeanor either.

These men, infirm of purpose, slaves to the spirit of exploitation are but the beasts we will redeem our world of… Rise O Noble ones and let us march with the heads of these imposters to the **Valley of Ignorants** where awaits our Lord the true GOD..."

The "Fatwa" was a rude awakening that scared and angered me at the same time.

How could Laura do this? Would She actually reach out for my throat? Behead me? Where did the fallen Lucifer find the true GOD?

But there was no time to waste and this unsuspecting uprising had to be curbed before it took preposterous proportions.

The more I think of it the more I know my Waterloo awaits me in the **Valley of Ignorance** and the discomfort only grows. And yet, this intoxicated GODHOOD would make my feelings numb and veil my frailties when Laura the fallen angel pays for her revolt.

I summon **Mucus** and **Moron** in a hurriedly convened meeting to put to rest the anxiety of sudden turn of events.

A meeting is convened by the sleaze party at the city center, which in its poetic justice scares the crows and pigeons away from the morbid apparition of **Callous.** And tonight, he shall be cleaned and garlanded again. We need another reason to prove ourselves worthy of his sacrifice.

Moron has already circulated pamphlets declaring a reward on Laura and anyone who would be associated with her. Her " Fatwa" has most conveniently been reworded as a secret letter that the **Amphibiotic Ambivalents** would have sent to her to dislodge the Lord of the valiant **Marsh Dwellers** and rob them of their new meaning, of their Lord... and their authority.

The faithfuls of the sleaze party will hold Laura captive in her own fort tonight. So she would not have a chance to defend herself even as her **Noble Warriors** succumb to the charisma of Norman Pinglepop and the farce of **Moron** tonight.

Somewhere I am not convinced that Laura needs to die. I still hold my argument that there is no GOD without the eternal Lucifer.

And now that we had successfully pre-empted her revolt, it has done us more good than bad. The ferocious **Noble Warriors** are now the most ardent followers of their Lord Norman Pinglepop for lack of another authority to drive their raw power.

For my part, Norman Pinglepop, the blissfully patronizing and eternally forgiving father has taken them in his fold without as much as a word. After all, **Moron** would make a suitable story out of it, to arouse their guilt and unflinching trust of the common masses in me (read Norman Pinglepop).

It did me a great favor because for all these days, I was unable to find a suitable General to march on the **Ambivalents** and now I have the **40 Noble Warriors** to lead the attack under the able leadership of **Mucus,** who has spread enough sleaze among the **Ambivalents** already.

For their part, the **Ambivalents,** I am told, were taken by surprise at the sudden turn of events in God's country. Now, they have evolved their own genre of guilt and witch-hunting.

Somewhere, they so wish to admire the man who would instigate Laura -the noblest Angel and yet, on the other hand, they would rather have him burnt to death on the city square for fear of inviting the wrath of Norman Pinglepop.

This alas! Has always been their bane. The **Ambivalents** were always torn between the two extremes-the ones who wanted to live and those who plain existed and had often been on strife.

While **Mucus** has been actively spreading the dual sleaze of fear and contempt for the **Marsh Dwellers** among the **Ambivalents**, **Moron** has been feeding them with false hopes of reconciliation with the supreme Lord Norman Pinglepop. This will help us catch them unawares and before they realize their plight, they would assume our attack as a supreme punishment for their misdeeds.

This dichotomy ho! I had always thought that the **Ambivalents** would fall easy, given their own diametrically opposite confusions but that is easier said then done. They do deserve a place in the annals of history as a race that went down fighting.

After all, the **Marsh Dwellers** would be disappointed in their Lord for having won over a weak foe, when he could have easily harnessed them to servitude without bloodshed.

Besides, I can see the growing power of **Mucus** and somewhere, he has to find his watery grave in the **Amphibiatic valley,** where generations could feed on his sleaze and produce the single cell disasters that later generations of conditioning can eulogize as the life giving single celled wonders.

Also, the **Noble Warriors** are infirm of purpose and always seeking a better leader to follow.

They deserve martyrdom for robbing Laura of her moment of honor. Yet they are too dangerous to come back alive.

Today I will christen **Mucus** as the leader of our "Mission Annihilation". The idea is to strike before remorse or pity takes the better of our people, and before the **Ambivalents** fall prostrate on our feet in exchange for simple mediocre living with some crumbs of security to ensure their permanence on the geography of an unknown planet. What life! And here I am going to give them a heroic death! I am indeed a true Lord.

Mucus with his sleaze army will lead the bastion from front and the **Noble Warriors** will protect his victory March from behind. The **Ambivalents** will be taken by surprise, and true to their name, they will still be contemplating between the valor of the nobles and the sleaze of **Mucus,** when they would be struck.

Inactivity has often fuelled their arguments and witch-hunting has been their reward. After the war is over, the handful of them left will also find reason for the rest of their lives while no reason would be right. After all, this ambivalence is the hallmark of their existence.

Moron has been really helpful in fuelling fear in **Mucus.** He was able to propagate the fear of Laura regrouping among the **Ambivalents,** to take her revenge on his sleaze party.

Moron was able to successfully substantiate his claim by beheading the loyalists of **Mucus** in Laura's camp and sending them as a gift to **Mucus,** as though it had been sent by Laura. The message underneath a dripping sword soaking blood read, " My sword is hungry for more and she awaits you".

That night before his final departure **Mucus** had come to me and I shared his grave doubts about Laura and the gift sent to him. But it was too late.

He had to go now, not only in service to his Lord but to avenge his faithful. His spleen and gall both must have told him that something was amiss that night. But sometimes reason is subservient to valor and both, often at times are exclusive to each other in their blinded obedience.

What he had done to **Callous** now seemed to be his own faith and **Mucus** could barely hide his contempt for his Lord and the mean **Moron** with his propaganda machine…or so I would have thought.

But like all tales of invincibility that we breed around us, and hope for eternity to us, even as we see corpses falling around us, **Mucus** was consumed that night with his new found passion of avenging his fellow men.

Before sunset, Laura had to sacrifice her head held high in pride to his sword, which he would present to his Lord.

"**Callous** was, after all, stupid and it was me, **Mucus** who had made him the king of men. He had to go, but I will stay because I am the kingmaker".

While the **Nobles** always doubted the capability of **Mucus** to lead from the front, they had resigned to the supreme command of their Lord the legendary Norman Pinglepop.

And for my part, Norman Pinglepop, did not come out of his palace to greet his army, the final speck of honor.

Moron was to represent him this day and declare that he the Lord will only leave his palace to welcome the victorious army of **Mucus** and the **Noble Warriors.** Till then Norman Pinglepop will spend time in prayers for the betterment of this war ravaged planet and the plight of the millions who suffer from incessant grief and trauma caused by the ambitious likes of Laura and the **Mosquitoers,** and now the treachery of the **Ambivalents**.

Mucus led his valiant attack from the front while true to their words, the **Noble Warriors** provided support at the rear.

Our calculations hit the target right and **Ambivalents** were indeed helter-skelter, still trying to make up their mind if they should face **Mucus** squarely in the front, or take on the **Noble Warriors** from behind and then surprise **Mucus** too, from the rear.

Mucus swooned upon the hapless **Ambivalents** till he was within striking distance of their city center, where he would flag the authority of his Lord Norman Pinglepop.

He stood at the city center. His moment of truth had arrived. He looked down at the fighting masses and for a moment, felt like a giant commandeering the pygmies under him.

For a moment he could not stop himself from comparing his valor to that of Norman Pinglepop. And in the next moment his existence was larger than his Lord, who indeed had fought no battle and hence was not half as much a man, as **Mucus.**

While the reverie created a false bastion of security around **Mucus** and the illusions of invincibility once again took the better of him, an arrow struck him in the eye.

He had just enough time to see the woman who had spoilt his victory and she looked like Laura. He cried out loud and hence gave the finishing touches to **Moron**'s master plan.

The loud " Laura" from their falling captain filled the victorious army with a gloom never before seen. The foes and friends alike could not fathom how would Laura be in the battle field and yet not be noticed by any till the time she would strike?

The truth never dawned that there was no Laura! There was no time to be wasted in trying to find the truth. The **Ambivalents** were yet again lost in their duality of success... that of having found a scapegoat and the comfort and that of having lost it. And this would once again give them eternal reason for survival-one that will fuel their guilt for having inflicted such harm to the holy soldiers of the Lord Norman Pinglepop.

This guilt will help them live in thralldom and servile fearfulness of the mighty Lord, now that they had a reason to blame it all on them. And, on the other hand, they would rejoice because the mighty **Mucus** had fallen in the gory battle of the **Ambivalents**.

They would be able to find solace and reason in their textbooks of history, about the great deeds of their forefathers, and how they had almost won a battle, which was eventually lost. Because the truth can be misdirected, but the results can seldom be overturned.

Anyways, I am happy they will find their reasons. Their pre-occupation is indeed important for me to handle the uprisings at home, now that Lucifer assumes the power of a heretic to find his usual fan following.

To start with, **Moron** has provided grounds to yet again commit to a long night of daggers in the garb of Laura.

Mucus' body with the Victory March is being led home by the remaining **Noble Warriors.**

The Victory March will be led straight to the city center where next to **Callous'** statue, **Mucus** will find his humble abode in stone and crow droppings.

The **Marsh Dwellers** are now well rehearsed in the grief and celebrations of a mixed victory and although heroes in majority are not fancy anymore, they would still find their reasons to celebrate as long as the alcohol and guilt of being free post intoxication is fed into their systems by **Moron** and their Lord Norman Pinglepop.

I have a ploy that will take care of the **Noble Warriors** too. I might be getting paranoid but I think they need to die too. Not that their death would serve much purpose. But then, certain things are also done for the pure pleasure of play.

Besides when my beloved Lucifer, Laura hears of the brutal dismemberment of her loyal few, would not her eyes cry blood? Sometimes this self obsessed Narcissism scares me but most of the times I am quite comfortable with it. After all, no authority is perennial and especially not a borrowed one. So I need to make the best of it as long as it lasts.

At the city center, as the celebrating masses garland their fallen hero, **Mucus,** amidst tears and alcohol, I would arrive at the scene.

I will declare the **Noble Warriors** culprits for not being able to save the lives of the heroic **Mucus**. The selected loyalists of the sleaze party will then fall upon the **Noble Warriors,** dismembering each of them with brutal heartlessness.

I fear bedlam will break lose in the city. And in the mayhem anything can happen. But then I am also sure that my **Marsh Dwellers** will discover a newfound savagery in them, wherein they would join the headless mob of the sleaze workers to tear the **Noble Warriors** apart for their deception.

I plan to execute the sleaze workers thereafter, for having done this harm unto the great nation of their Lord for war and crimes are but a necessity that should not be resorted to. And the best time to educate them of this limited right is post action.

Moron looks at me with a scared look of a dove now in captivity, now playing with its master in harmony.

My sinister design for ones scared him too. I can see the burning question in his eyes, "Will I be next?" But I pre-empt that before I am forced with the truth.

"**Moron** my friend, you are the most loyal of my subjects and it's on you that all authority rests. You will live a hundred years to serve thy master in right earnest and your name will be etched in gold for your unwavering service to this great nation.".

Convinced of his invincibility, **Moron** walks out of the portico with confident swagger and heads straight for his task.

His propaganda machinery had alternatively made heroes and villain out of the sleaze workers and **Noble Warriors,** so that utmost mayhem would follow when the sleaze workers are summarily executed.

Everything went as per plan and I allow myself indulgence in my senses today for the great feat accomplished today.

I will walk up to the city center and address my people.

I will have tears for the dead in the Great War and words of caution for the living. I will have words for praise for the **Nobles** and adequate admonition too.

I will praise the sleaze worker for their role in the war that the ever-famous **Callous** had won, and their victory over the **Ambivalents** and I will desecrate them for playing havoc on the **Noble Warriors** who were such reformed criminals.

I can already hear the praises of " Hail our Lord Norman Pinglepop" outside my door. And that means my time has come to go fill my **sheep** with a sense of purpose, a sense of direction and enough intoxication to live a hundred lifetimes in non-questioning numbness and loyalty to a cause they would never know, because they would never qustion.

The victory speech by **Moron** I am told, was well done. My authority assumed a new high.

But there is not time to be wasted in past glory. I have realized this of late… *the larger we grow, the larger we need to grow to keep the unrestricted stature alive.* Sometimes I really wonder if I am a GOD to pull this off but I know still that something lurks in the **Valley of Ignorants**.

Laura, I am told, now takes refuge among the **Ignorants**. Yet she is not attempting another uprising against me. A known devil is always better then an unknown one I am told… but this devil speaks no more and I know from experience that a quiet thinking devil is the best foe to have.

I also have to find a suitable conclusion for **Moron** while he still holds my authority supreme. He has grown too powerful and much to my dismay he is still comfortably out of public view. He has learnt the perils of popularity and prefers his role as a kingmaker. This leaves me with little choice but to make a martyr of him and in the absence of a cause I will not be able to cleanse my **Marshy** populace of his sinister presence.

These are troubled days and now, as the end of the Great War faces me squarely, I am not sure if **Moron** should lead the attack on **Ignorants**.

After all, no propaganda is effective without blind knowledge and the sense of justice provided by the blind lady. Hence he, will be ineffective there.

Besides, Laura has been there for long and I do not, for a change, know the moves of my opponents. Besides, I am also not sure if **Moron** can be trusted alone in the Valley with Laura to win them over.

I will have to lead the final assault and **Moron** will have to be banished before that.

I spend long nights planning my move but things seem to be on a standstill now.

I am yet to find out what would drive the **Ignorants**? Will the presence of an almighty GOD himself be of help? But do they believe in GODHOOD... or did they ever do?

Sometimes I wonder if it would be a good idea to retrace my path to the forests, now that I have tasted my mouthful of sky as Norman Pinglepop. After all, how long will I be able to carry this farce and to what end?

Would it not be better to leave the battle midway and live in a glory of what could have been for the rest of the lives of **Marshy** Dwellers? I still got my reverence and I still got my GODHOOD and their Lord can always take a new form with a new sunrise.

But power comes for a price- a price that consumes the creator. And no matter how strong the logic of being a surviving martyr, the visions of ultimate glory and eternal victory still hold me captive.

I am sure my Laura will return to me someday. This time, I will look at her face too and then take her away. She will forgive my farce and we will live happily ever after.

I am glad **Moron** walked in my room that night to break these self-destructive thoughts that are often a balm for a fearful heart.

He has a plan and though it seems a little clichéd, I think there is vitue in it.

Now that I look back, it was not a plan that **Moron** had got for me- just a little piece of information that had perplexed him. In that vain moment of wanting to pledge his allegiance to Norman Pinglepop, when you hear of a popular revolt somewhere else and your sycophancy gets the better of you.

"My Lord the Holy God", Laura has betrayed her people. She has betrayed her pledge. How much I wished to show her the grave when she had dared to revolt against her God but your goodness alas! And now I am told, she is breeding another God among the **Ignorants**."

Laura indeed was getting smarter and this did not augur well for me, I thought in the first breath till I realized that all she was doing was to facilitate my game.

Voltaire's God I am sure is a creation of her little mind. How else would **Ignorants** ever be such an aware breed?

Sometimes I marvel at her ingenuity and at others, her perseverance. To be able to make the **Ignorants** wake up to the knowledge that does not dirty your spleen? A people's God as he liked to call himself I was told… and all that is holy and subservient, commanding in me was but his strength in anti-thesis.

I had reasons to be wild at this unusual turn of events. My fledgling faculties now lost in intoxication, now lost in power had little left by way of sanity and all these days I had spent in pensive melancholy trying to clear my path of **Moron** and win over the **Ignorants.** And yet not a thought worth the sanction of action has occurred to me yet.

And here stands Laura, with a new trouble for me. And now I could not rest in past laurels either because I am convinced if I do not make the first move, Laura will come looking for my blood in thirst and haste.

I think I was weird that evening with **Moron**. Could he have seen the fear in my eyes? or did he peep in to the crypts of an evil design to which he might soon fall victim? Sly has a way with men… the best of the actors fall to the charm of that evil smile that veils the lips of a thinking cynic.

Moron recommends that instead of tact and diplomacy which had been the hallmark of all bloodless coups and bloody battles fought by **Marsh Dwellers** in the name of honor for their brethren and cleansing the evil of their foes, we make an all out attack on the **Ignorants** and capture them by beheading **Voltaire's God** and calling his farce in the open.

"He wants me to have an open debate on the virtues of Godhood where **Moron** feels confident that I will be able to establish the superior Godhood and make eternal the **Marshy** Dwellers."

The plan on the face of it seems commendable. Just that I have learned over the years that any strategy of strike is only as good as the authenticity of information from the enemy camp and I am going to rest my case till **Moron** can feed me information on the changes at the **Valley of Ignorants.** And till such time, he gets me the statistics of popularity and the enchantment of **Voltaire's God.**

Sometimes I wonder how people can be so stupid in their eternal wisdom and more so, how do they lead themselves to blind following to their own execution?

Moron is an asset when it comes to his devotion to me. But my insecurity and hunger are not compatible with his existence. He has to go but not before I am sure I have the wherewithal to take on the **Ignorants** and their newfound osession... Call it God.

I had a good night sleep and it's morning again. I have summoned **Moron** to discuss the modus operandi to create an effective spy network feeding on the propaganda press of **Moron**. Since the time **Mucus** met his martyrdom, **Moron** has been looking after the sleaze army and has been able to effectively convert it into a spy network using his propaganda army for cover.

He has been able to suppress many an uprisings in the **Mountain Mosquitoers** and **Amphibiotic Ambivalent** on the strength of timely information, which his establishment feeds him with.

Since a God cannot be king, he has been heading the empire created out of the tiny **Marsh Dwellers** and has been eternally grateful to me for bestowing this honour on him.

For my part, there is ill ease because power corrupts and he sure is malleable by any long strand of hair, which might decide to tie him. After all, every man has his moment of weakness and that one vice, which is his grave… so also with **Moron**? Indeed! Sometimes I fear that he has put the entire machinery in place to feed his Lord Norman Pinglepop with the events at The **Valley of Ignorants**.

True to his reputation he has been feeding the Valley with the farce of their newfound God and the virtues of original Godhood in Norman Pinglepop. The **Ignorants** who have had their first brush with knowledge also seem to be responding to the game and that gives me some breather.

I am hoping to pierce the logic and reputations of **Voltaire's God** with the poison that **Moron** brews and then challenge him to a duel of words, where he would fall weak and lowly to my feet.

There are two kinds of freedom. The true freedom, where we do what we ought to do and the illusionary freedom where we do what we wish to do. In the latter, we are often enslaved to the pleasures of our senses and the web of our conditioning and hence what is often acted upon is that which suits us in ill- taste.

This however, is not visible to the naked eye as it is often dressed in fancy and eulogized in the garb of sacrifice, martyrdom, heroism, chivalry and all else fancy sounding expressions.

I have often wondered at the futility of patriotism dependent on simply protecting the borders of a state while allowing all acts of treason and adultery to be committed inside those realms.

Would I respond to the call for sacrifice when I know that all I am expected to be is but a poor feedstock for someone's ambition here or foolery there? And yet the world is agog with the stories of those who live and die for the sake of physical boundaries even as they themselves fall prey to the deterioration in values and morals within.

In the light of this ill- fitting freedom, how is it that man has given up on thinking? To still romanticize a zombie's existence, ha, alas!

This false freedom then forms the basis of power. The power that plays on the sentiment and rules by the brawn of a dying head, devoid of reason and oblivious to the bounty that he hides under a bushel so well.

The comfort of numbness goes a long way in making lives miserable and then in the honest attempt at witch hunting, fate is the next casualty in the blame game.

How many times I had heard… "But how can I fight fate, if this is what my God destines for me, so be it." This resignation is an ocean of patience; sometimes insurmountable by even life and many a soul are known to have found their crypts in this belittled existence of fate.

Meager as it is in singularity, as a mob this sentiment can overthrow Gods and cults and reinstate new orders on unassuming men.

I am told, that the **Ambivalents** in their restless indecision had ones created a great order for themselves, which gave them the power to rule both land and water. And then, they could not decide where they belonged. From a uniform empire they had created and where they could occupy an entire planet, they started to segregate water bodies from land bodies. Slowly half their brethren sacrificed the art of water dwelling for a dedicated land life and some other factions chose waters over land.

The well meaning few persisted on both land and water and were termed heretics till their number dwindled to a minority.

They had great leader once or was it the common power of conviction? But they staged a coup to regain their past glory. Unfortunately, the coup was suppressed, not by a unified opposition of the land dwellers or the water dwellers. Not before they managed a compromise and hence are the lone surviving bastions of a past glory.

They saw their glory bite dust, as the land dwellers and the water dwellers divided themselves and subdivided themselves till their were a thousand factions of each, some warring, some compromising. All in all, living a mockery for life and game for purpose till they would die in singularity and praise their belittling race in a mob again.

The Ambivalent who had started with the heroic lust soon lost their pomp and valor which often happens when basic survival takes the better of a thinking race, and were lead to mediocrity and thereafter oblivion, till they woke up to their new God, the mighty Norman Pinglepop.

I am told that when the social order during the reign of terror and the great war of micro independence was being fought, the intellectuals of that era were busy defacing the truth of their opponents.

The unfortunate developments borne out of political regroupings and convenience often found these intellects at loggerheads with themselves. They would no more stand up to their own word since what they slander today, would be their loyalty's call tomorrow.

The social order seemed to be breaking down. The ambivalent were the most distraught race and how they saw the glory of their erstwhile brethren fall to grave!

One such infidel amongst them I am told was **Voluptuous Voltaire**. **Voltaire** was a man of supreme conviction and not without grounding that any form of life is dependent on just two eternal wells of life-Love and Fear.

Love demands harmony. It requires trust. Love believes in the highest order of self-discipline and love is unconditional. In short, Voltaire would say, "Love is an illusion."

It does not nurture ambition but where it is meant as a sacrifice to the love. It does not nurture ego because Love is to lose the false sense of identity. Love is bad for commerce and trade since it is unconditional. By this very vice Love is unfit for the society.

When I first found the hypothesis of Voltaire in reckless abandon at a dying museum after my victory over the **Ambivalents** I was amused... surprised... confused...pensive. "How can such wisdom be condemned to dark dingy corners of a lost land? And yet, as I was thinking about it, the most formidable of my enemies came to my mind- the **Ignorants** and all was clear to me in that moment of bright light passing through my veins. In priesthood, it is called the moment of wisdom... in my case, borrowed wisdom.

Voltaire had elaborated on the futility of Love for society and commerce. He held that basic tenet of un-conditionality as the bane of this supreme emotion.

Based on un- conditionality Love is anti- commerce and hence anti- capitalism and hence anti-growth and hence anti-development and hence anti social.

Love dissuades ambition and hence limits the potential to which mankind and animal kind together can be exploited to yield best barter for money that was solely created for the purpose of bartering with ease. Hence, love diminishes the halo of man's greatest creation; money which breeds on ambition.

Love is selfless and does not distinguish between the sinner and the noble. That in a stroke robs any thinking man the medals of chivalry, valor, and superiority, success, which anyways is relative and hence needs someone to be fodder for its survival. But that apart, Love by being selfless is criminal in its philosophy of equality, which is a good thought but a poor tool of execution.

Imagine the chaos without power. We do need a few good men to divide for the collective whole of the world. To think of it, my own power depends on this and my unscrupluousity is not a unique invention. It exists across thankless brains, which much to your chagrin, is a majority.

Voltaire realized that love cannot be a motivator and that it will never be accepted in a material driven society where conditioning rules the thoughtless minds.

Yet, having established a seat of power to comprehend the social fabric, which we live in, what could rule a man?

So it was fear then that won the battle by elimination. Fear indeed has all the right ingredients to command sacrifice.

To earn fear are battles waged, to live fear are tyrants praised, to spread fear are martyrs raised… fear alas! The fearful wombs create.

Fear can govern a life in pursuit of accepting it and unleashing it. Fear makes relativity a standard unto itself and the hordes we command shall now govern the success of existence.

But that one flaw in relative fear still needed attention. An ultimate point source of fear had to be invented. That which shall have rebellion and the rebellion shall be crushed with the vagaries of time and stories shall be woven into garments to hide the degenerating life. We will call our heroes martyrs and change the breath to killers in another place at another time and as though its own prophecy, relativity shall create the world in black and white and the semblance of grey shall be lost to sight.

Fear would then take garb of love and all that is bad and worse shall now be the harlot of our dear love… And need in sex shall rule the night and intoxicated souls always on a high, shall count the countless dying hearts and make an army ready to charge… they will cry in grief at what they have lost and surrender to another moment of pleasure till the fire is lost.

The guilt shall play the gullible host. In collective, we laugh and alone the swore shall show. Life will be a statistic and the count of pleasures-a gift, we shall live in freedom to infringe the weak and fear shall govern the equation of the powerful free and the suffering weak.

So fear it is then that shall rule the roost and the ultimate in fear shall be the name we choose. We call it God, he shall be revered, he shall be feared and love shall take the blame and fear shall call the shots.

Thus was created **Voltaire's God.**

I remember that night… it was long indeed and I could not sleep. **Voltaire** had seen what we live and in oblivion he died for there was none by his side. They feared him, called him mad and when he died, they celebrated in joy. The grey cells are now buried with his corpse, the final dying gift to the dead soul of their erstwhile God.

I was lost in thought about the Voltaire's God and now a strange fear gripped me. How did Laura find out about him and how did she resurrect the mighty God now asleep with his ideals in an unsung grave and create a halo around him amongst the **Ignorants**?

Nobody loves a fallen hero and hence when the original Norman Pinglepop had taken a flight to the forest, I had to be christened with his name for the fear that his glory might be lost to oblivion and my **Marsh Dwellers** would be left with no God willing to abide by their pathetic disposition called life.

Voltaire's God is a fallen hero but I realize his ideals will dress a new slate yet untouched by conditioning better… Was my Lucifer so smart? Could my Laura identify this basic tenet amongst the **Ignorants** before I could see it?

Oh! How I hope I had thought about it and then I could be the undisputed leader of the **Ignorants**…

Yet my fear of the **Valley of Ignorants** has only grown with this realization and **Voltaire's God** is now as much a reality as this Norman Piglepop.

Moron comes running to my room. He has information for me and I have disdain for him. In any case my disdain does not ride on my ego, and so, I often tolerate him well. Besides, he feeds me with good information- timely and effective.

His color is pale with fear and paler with anxiety. He reiterates, “Had not I told you, Laura should die?” I can sense the urgency of his concern but I do not like his tone any better.

The next few hours, that night, **Moron** described to me how the **Ignorants** had set aside their lethargy to the fireplace of their cold hearts and headed to the streets to welcome their Lord- **Voltaire’s God.**

Laura the fallen angel was the accomplice in this crime and credible sources have it that she was instrumental in creating this awareness.

Laura, I am assuming would have had access to the same privy information on the **Ambivalents** as I did, given the **Noble Warriors**. I am sure none survived in my event of things but in such things, one can really never be too sure.

“She outsmarted me in this game I thought. She went ahead and created a new God. I was so full of appreciation for her and her perseverance. Betrayed by her own Lord

Norman Pinglepop, banished from her state for attempting to do good to her people and here she was, the same die-hard old conformist demanding the rightful honors that her lover, the real Norman Pinglepop deserved and by the same virtue she deserved."

Moron tells me that she had resurrected the sleeping genius of the **Ignaorants** and fed them on past laurel of their ancestors.

She had told them vague stories about a unified world and how the **Amphibians** had indulged in their destruction get-together during times of peace, and how the consummations in pleasures had led to the great divide of the world. The way the mariners were born and how the land dwellers came by, and how finally mariners and the land dwellers divided the world and subdivided the world, till it was a congregation of petty states that kept fighting with each other.

She had told them of the divine revenge when God was disposed from the world and his rights as the creator were relinquished in favor of the piecemeal constituencies of a few powerful and striving creatures.

The **Ignorants** had slept to this great truth and would have continued to frustrate Laura's effort, but when they heard about their great ancestors, the **Ambivalents,** and how they had tried to protect the world, the tables started to turn and the efforts of Laura had started to bear results.

The **Ignorants** by virtue of being ignorant had forgotten what could have induced such a stupendous stupor in them.

The plight of the **Ambivalents** had been reduced to rubble and that never inspired confidence. But the events leading to their indecisive existence sure scared the **Ignorants** and filled them with fear.

They wanted to fight the stupor away and start to think again. Laura made me the advocate of the same doctrines of power and fear that had gotten their ancestors to this plight and played well on the breaking sensibilities of the **Ignorants** to make me a villain.

What had been left incomplete in the volumes of Voltaire's that I lay my hands on, I realized had landed into Laura's hand.

While the virtues of fear as a means to rule that did suit my purpose was with me, the virtues of Love somehow evaded me.

I was amazed at how Laura could imbibe fear amongst the **Ignorants** and use that to breed Love among their brethren and for their God, while using the same energies to target their hatred towards me. "What a balancing act", I thought..." Indeed! Energy in the world is constant and what goes aound comes around."

Now that I look back, I realize how stupid I had been with that idea of a duel. I mean facing **Voltaire's God** was Fear facing Love, and legends have it that never has Fear looked Love in the eye.

But like all consummations, power has its blind spots too.

In a fit of rage, that night I had proclaimed to **Moron** my desires of taking on the **Ignorants** and their newfound awakening head on.

I sent **Moron** to the **Valley of Ignorants** with a message for Laura to surrender and come back to **Marshy** Land.

I was hoping that **Moron** will be able to relive the Love that Laura had for her Land and come back with her.

That would be an opportune moment for me to strike at **Moron** and proclaim him a traitor of the state for joining hands with the enemy. The fact that this was a secret mission would only go in my favor.

"And then the look in his eyes, that fear borne out of helpless hatred, that disgust of being a pawn to his own craft, the sudden outburst of guilt at having misled Laura and the eternal satisfaction that at least in his death he would be a hero in the eyes of Laura. Never mind the fact that she would be dying soon too…"

Sometimes my own cunning surprised me. How easy it was to convince **Moron** about my plan to lure Laura back to **Marsh Land** and then have her burnt alive for heresy. And how easily I was now in command of both their lives. I smiled to myself and while at other times, I would have given a day's rest to my stressed faculties, there was no time to be wasted today.

I was anxious, **Moron** had left after taking my blessings and he seemed the good old **Moron**…

Yet, I kept watching him for a long while as he diminished in size and finaly galloped out of sight.

It had been 2 weeks since **Moron** left on his errand and there was no news of him yet. I realized I had been depending on him a wee bit too much with local administration of the **Marsh Land**. I also ran the risk of being exposed to my adversaries in the wake of the falling effectiveness of the sleaze party in the absence of **Moron**.

There had been incidents of underground revolution, which was thankfully just a false alarm but it left me cold and shivering for the entire night.

Ultimate power also meant absolute vulnerability. And with all of my aides and adversaries being systematically eliminated I ran the risk of running out of enough "causes" to keep my martyr race alive.

And without the zeal their devotion to the supreme purpose of Godhood would also diminish.

A vain emptiness now started to grip me. What was there to my Godhood after the **Valley of Ignorants** would fall? This post orgasmic quiet often resembled a decaying city after the great deluge.

"The life giving water having flown out, what are left are the rubble and the garbage, and we the scavengers wanting to put the pieces together in the eternal wait for the next great downpour. How silly ha! And yet how purposeful in its micro existence. I am the God, the true

One and in my purposelessness follows an entire nation of thoughtless souls wanting to be heroes in their own collective rights, not for once wanting to think that that, which is collective is seldom unique and that which is not unique, often differentiable and that which cannot be differentiated, often mediocre.

My own wisdom is now the anathema of my actions. The empty vacant clamoring of power and more power now seem hollow and insignificant and this does not augur well for me in the wake of the impending duel with **Voltaire's God.**"

And then a thought strikes me. What if I give up on my Godhood and instead become a God maker? I could run away from the **Marsh Land** back to the forests and leave a "Fatwa" behind, beckoning **Moron** and Laura to come back to their motherland and take the reigns. To carry on the legacy of their God unto eternity. I would have made a mark then, in my own inconspicuous existence, yet the glory that would shine posthumously shall be endearing.

Or I could make Godhood unique by being that perfect signature of sacrifice and content by refusing to face another God. I shall prove that all Gods are but one and their incarnations do not suffer from petty insecurities to force them into a duel.

I shall proclaim that the legacy left by Norman Pinglepop shall henceforth be carried by **Voltaire's God**... and that there is no distinction among Gods but in mortals who have already been won to the side of good by myself in the holy wars of the **Mosquitoers** and the **Ambivalents**.

Now that the **Ignorants** are also waking up to knowledge, my surprise will augur well with the wisdom of their disposition and that will spare me the pain of a duel while still helping me maintain the supreme Godhood of Norman Pinglepop.

Laura will be frustrated in her own efforts and will relent to her failures in the obvious garb of success.

Moron shall be left to the judgement of the people who shall tear him apart for all the misdoings unto the living, or they may spare him as a reformed criminal. In either case, his hatred for me shall show him the grave and his blindfolded worship will earn him a statue next to his worhy comrades, **Callous** and **Mucus.**

I was still lost in my reverie when a messenger walked in. He had a message for me from **Moron**. For a moment I skipped a beat. "What was a messenger doing here when **Moron** should have been here with Laura!"

Hiding the wavering tone behind a stoic composure, I asked him for the message which he delivered with no feelings or emotions.

I think I went pale because I could see it in the eyes of the messenger. He must have been anticipating seeing me all happy at having got an invitation for a duel with **Voltaire's God**. He must have hoped to see his God swell with pride at yet another opportunity to prove his supremacy but my looks betrayed any texture of confidence.

All my plans for once had been pre-empted. The stage was set for the Gods to face each other and the end result would prove one to be a farce and the other would stay supreme. The odds by sheer number and quantum of territory under my control were with me but only I have known the eternal war of fear and love and the age-old superstition scared me at that moment.

The invitation to the duel sounded like a death knell but I had to keep my courage alive and face the consequences of my own creation.

I could not hope for a peaceful retirement by appointing my successor and live in the past plaudits and glory of my assumed self. I had to fight and prove my supremacy.

I still had hope wherein a few early salvos would put me in the position of strength and then I could stop the duel midway and let my fallen foe be my benefactor, the carrier of my torch to spread the message of Godhood.

I think it is decided. This is going to be my plan. To overwhelm **Voltaire's God** with a few well-chosen blows at the outset. Then hold his hand and lead him to my own crown. He has to be the martyr for my cause and in my nobility will live the rest of humanity, sometimes in awe, sometimes in hatred, and often times in absolute ignorance of their menial self, often used as haystacks to create fires where there were none warranted.

My confidence is on a high this day. I am headed towards the **Valley of Ignorants** where I will appoint my successor. **Moron** my old faithful shall be there too and he shall either fall prostrate at the grandeur of his master or become the gift from Norman Pinglepop to **Voltaire's God** to run an efficient administration over the unified community of living creatures, brought under one roof by the visionary God, their Lord, Norman Pinglepop.

Laura, I am hoping will be overcome by love and repentance for her Lord, Norman Pinglepop whom she had doubted in the past, and this way, I am hoping I will finally get a chance to take her to bed. My eternal desire to see her in close proximity bare to the core had been draped by the need to be all powerful and omnipresent and now that I shall be the undisputed God of the territory. All my subjects shall be at my behest- masters and slaves as I would proclaim them to be and Laura should be no exception.

The prospects of the day unfolding to the cues of my master plan seem promising and that lends immense confidence to my gait as I partake my slow elephant mounted march to the **Valley of Ignorants**.

I am prepared with my opening speech. I have ruled with the iron fist and filled my people with a sense of purpose hitherto missing.

In my severity their was a reward of perseverance and in my oppression the need for discipline that now binds together the entire colony from the **Marsh Lands** to the Mountains to the Rivers and the Valleys.

For fear is what has governed the world and the iron fist has maintained the order. For man in his eternal destruction get together, needs a God to save him from the sin and deliver him from hell and alike all actions that are but slaves of the eternal action reaction climax-anticlimax, so is the Godhood of their Lord Norman Pinglepop, at once threatening and at once, the eternal purpose of their very existence.

I can envision the stadium full of people in anticipation and they're at yonder, a pale fledgling **Voltaire's God** standing to bow to the bounty of the almighty Norman Pinglepop. I can see **Moron** standing by the door to receive his Lord, and Laura trying to be the last straw of hope to her unfinished portrait (read **Voltaire's God).**

Much to my chagrin, there is no **Moron** to receive me at the gate and when I finally see him, he is holding a mike announcing the commencement of the duel.

I do have reasons to be wild at him but when I hear him pronounce my name to begin the great verbal duel, I am impressed with his presence of mind. Else, I would have never succeeded in my plan to be the savior of the savior.

Moron shall be rewarded for his good deed and his unflinching devotion to me. I can see his sly speaking from his eyes as he acknowledges my appreciation for his presence of mind here.

I begin with the power of knowledge, which the Valley is still Ignorant about and the virtues of fear to ensure order in the lives of ordinary mortals.

I recount the text I had found at the **Ambivalents** and eulogize the virtues of fear as the sustaining power that differentiates man from God.

The thunderous applause from the audience fills the place when I complete my comprehension of the ancient text of which, Laura has the missing part and just when I start to take my initial steps towards a shivering **Voltaire's God** to declare the unity in the God's world, I hear the sermons on the power of love for the sustenance of Godhood.

It is my own **Moron**, speaking the missing links of **Voltaire's God** and Laura stands next to him in her benevolent best.

My feet start to lose all strength as I see the multitude slowly realize the gravity of those words that had often impressed me in person but scared my seat of power with their blatant honesty.

I realized that fear indeed cannot look eye to eye at love and as the lines from behind the scenes make their mark on the ignorant minds, the collective starts to scare me in the form of that mob which I see moving towards me.

In a moment of weakness, **Moron** speaks the entire treachery of his Lord Norman Pinglepop. In one breath, he demands the rationale for the martyrdom of **Mucus** and **Callous** and the **Nobles** and as each layer of that curtain unfolds, I see my own naked self being exposed further....

The moments now seem like years, I cannot walk any further. My strength gives way and I fall to the ground not very far from the feet of **Voltaire's God** that now reflects the power of the collective wish

When I regain my conscience it must have been a while because I see a huge sea of people heading towards me. From the look of it, they don't seem one bit friendly and yet in all that commotion I can hear the words I say...

"I am not Norman Pinglepop! I am not Norman Pinglepop…

But does it matter anymore to the hungry hounds. For them I am Norman Pinglepop and now they will pounce on me and tear my skin, suck my blood and cast my intestines away for the lesser dogs to pray…

Fear & Love… the two most potent emotions that have come to govern the human mind over the centuries are also the most common cause of confusion shrouding pretty much every social institution created by the society. Effortlessly flowing from one to the other, all endeavors at control are often an attempt to display fear under the garb of love, be it in personal relations or social aggregations. Norman Pinglepop is an attempt to segregate the motives of these two very powerful and conflicting drivers of world energy so one can choose allegiance only where it is due… to the emotion of LOVE.